Tanya looked up, still dazed by her ordeal. Her expression quickly turned from relief to horror at the sight before her.

"Ka-zar, it's Karl!" she shouted. "Stop him—before it's too late!"

"Witless woman," croaked a horrible voice, "it is already too late!"

That voice—it came from Karl Lykos! He now stood up and turned to face her. Archangel lay on the ground beneath him, turning human before her eyes—while the man she loved, Karl Lykos, was transformed into—a monster: half man, half pteranodon!

X-Men in the Savage Land

adapted by Paul Mantell and Avery Hart

cover illustration by Dana and Del Thompson

text illustrations by Aristides Ruiz

based on a story by Chris Claremont

Bullseye Books

Random House New York

A BULLSEYE BOOK PUBLISHED BY RANDOM HOUSE, INC.

Library of Congress Catalog Card Number: 94-67448
ISBN: 0-679-86700-7
RL: 3.0

Manufactured in the United States of America   10 9 8 7 6 5 4 3 2 1

X-MEN

X-Men in the Savage Land

PROLOGUE

· ·

The desert winds buffeted the helicopter as it navigated the twisted canyons and steep buttes of the American Southwest. The roar of the chopper's engine was deafening, and it seemed like forever since there had been any sign of human habitation.

Tanya Anderssen looked down at the beautiful landscape. She was twenty-seven, wealthy, as intelligent as she was beautiful— and broken-hearted. All her hopes now rode on this trip. "How much further, pilot?" she asked, shouting to be heard.

"We're almost there, Ms. Anderssen," the pilot yelled back. "An' don't worry. If anyone can help you, Mr. Worthington can."

"He *has* to," Tanya replied, staring at the copy of *National Geographic* in her hands—the one with the photo of the prehistoric wilderness called the Savage Land on the cover.

"We've arrived, ma'am," the pilot told her as they cruised over another tall butte. Tanya drew in her breath sharply at the sight of Warren Worthington's mountaintop chalet. It was truly magnificent! "Best view in these parts," the pilot informed her as they settled to the pad.

An attractive, dark-haired woman in a bikini came up from the pool area. "That's Candy Southern," the pilot told Tanya. "The boss's lady."

The two women greeted each other, and then Tanya looked around anxiously. "Where's Mr. Worthington?" she asked. "Please—I must see him right away."

"You will," Candy said kindly. "As for where he is—he's up visiting some friends."

Tanya looked up and saw three huge eagles circling overhead. No, wait—only two were eagles. The third was…a man!

But Warren Worthington III was not exactly your average man—he was a mutant!

Sole heir to one of America's larger private fortunes, he had been your basic rich kid until he hit puberty—and sprouted wings.

Under the code name of Angel, he had helped to found the X-Men. An encounter with the evil mutant Apocalypse left him scarred—bearing metal wings and the new code name of Archangel. Now he was recovering—far from the turmoil of the X-Men's never-ending struggle against injustice.

"So long, Icarus,...Daedalus!" he called up to his winged friends as he landed.

After a leisurely brunch, Archangel was finally ready to hear about the purpose of Tanya's visit.

"I want you to help me find Karl Lykos," she told Archangel.

"Karl was a childhood friend," Tanya continued. "Then he became the man I love. I first met him in Tierra del Fuego, in South America, where he saved my life. In gratitude, my father raised Karl after Karl's own father died suddenly. Karl put himself through medical school and became a brilliant, though quite unorthodox, physician. But nothing he did could ever make him worthy—in my father's eyes—of my love.

"What neither of us knew was that Karl was living under a terrible curse.

"Karl was a man of science, fascinated by the workings of the natural world. To find out what was wrong with himself, Karl became the subject of his own research!

"I've read his notes. To live, he had to drain energy from other living beings. Finally, an overdose of such energy transformed him into a...m-monster: half dinosaur, half man, all evil. He christened this other self 'Sauron.' He tried to kill my father, fought the X-Men"— she added with a nod to Archangel—"then fled to his home in Tierra del Fuego after the decent—human—side of his personality won out over his demonic Sauron-self. There, rather than live with his incurable curse, he decided it would be better not to live at all.

"After that, no matter what I did or how hard I tried, I couldn't forget that Karl had become an energy vampire because of *me*."

"Because of you?" Candy repeated.

"You see," Tanya explained, "when we were children he'd been infected by pteranodons, a species of prehistoric flying dinosaur.

They are extinct almost everywhere—except Tierra del Fuego.

"I blame myself completely for Karl's infection. *I* mistakenly disturbed the pteranodons' nest. Karl tried to save me, but the dinosaurs attacked *him* instead, infecting him with the virus that eventually transformed him into Sauron! If I had only defied my father and stayed with Karl after he was infected, I could have helped him..."

"Life is full of ifs, Tanya," Archangel said. "But you can't change the past, so why keep needlessly tormenting yourself about it? As you yourself said, Karl Lykos is dead."

"That's what I thought," Tanya replied, "until I read this magazine article about the Savage Land. One photo in particular caught my eye. I checked with the editors. It was taken less than six months ago."

She showed the photo to Archangel and Candy. It pictured a group of men in loincloths. Next to them stood a gigantic saber-toothed tiger. A huge blond man rested his hand gently on the tiger's back.

"The man standing beside Ka-zar, lord of the Savage Land," Tanya told them, pointing to a dark-haired, bearded man standing next to the blond one, "is Karl Lykos. I want to go to the Savage Land to find him." Staring up into Warren Worthington's sympathetic eyes, she said solemnly, "I'd like you to come with me."

"You're crazy!" Archangel replied, leaping to his feet.

"If you agree," Tanya said, "I'll donate a million dollars to your favorite charity."

"My help isn't for sale, Ms. Anderssen," Archangel informed her. "Anyway, has it occurred to you that Lykos hasn't left the Savage Land because he hasn't wanted to leave? Perhaps he's made peace with himself—and his 'curse'—down there. He might even be happy. Why not let him be?"

"Because I love him. Long ago, he sacrificed himself to save me. Now I must repay his love—by saving him from himself."

Tanya gazed up at him with tears in her eyes, her lower lip trembling with emotion. Determinedly, she pushed the hair from her eyes. "With or without your help...I'm going."

CHAPTER ONE

Welcome to the Savage Land

For a long moment there was silence. Then Archangel heaved a deep sigh. "Don't cry, Tanya, please," he begged. "I...I think I'm going to regret this. But an X-Man never turns down a request for help."

The next few days were busy ones, as Worthington pulled some strings and cashed in some IOU's to get clearances and government assistance for the trip to Antarctica, where the Savage Land was situated.

Finally, they were off. The two landed safely at the main American Antarctic base at McMurdo Sound. There they boarded a Navy helicopter, along with a pilot and co-pilot who were experienced in flying through the fierce winds of the freezing continent.

The chopper clawed its way eastward, toward the forbidding Eternity Mountains, which shielded the temperate climate of the Savage Land from the rest of the continent—and from the rest of the world.

"We're coming up on the Mist Wall, skipper," the co-pilot warned, referring to the layer of mist which habitually blanketed the Eternity Mountains. "Seems thicker than usual this trip. Good thing we laid in navigation beacons and a forward base."

"Seemed like the sensible thing to do, Sammy," the pilot replied, "what with all the traffic going in and out of the Savage Land these days."

Archangel sat listening to their conversation. Traffic into and out of the Savage Land? *Things sure have changed since I was here,* he reflected. Who knew—maybe this journey would go smoothly, with no complications, unlike the last time he was here, on a mission with the X-Men. He'd almost died that time...

Tanya, too, was lost in thought. She prayed she was doing the right thing. The odds against finding Karl were as huge as the Savage Land itself—but she had to try!

"Let's begin our descent, Sammy," the pilot said.

Suddenly, an inhuman shriek pierced the sky. "What the—?" the pilot said.

"A giant pteranodon!" the co-pilot shouted, pointing to the winged dinosaur heading straight for their craft. "It's too close, skipper! Look out! It's gonna *hit!*"

The beast slammed into them with the force of a missile. Pieces of rotor flew through the air.

"Everyone out!" the pilot yelled. "This baby's gonna blow!"

The first one out was Tanya—and she didn't jump. The chopper, tumbling earthward, had tilted on its side. Tanya fell though the open door—without a parachute!

In less than an instant, Archangel responded, swooping down on his powerful wings. "Just relax, Tanya," he called as he got

into position below her.

He grabbed her just as the chopper exploded, sending red-hot pieces of metal flying in a thousand directions.

Archangel had forgotten how big and nasty those pteranodons were. He wondered what was waiting for them on the ground.

Circling around, he saw that, fortunately, the pilot and co-pilot had gotten out in time. They were parachuting down through the mist, which had cleared off in their direction. Archangel stayed in the air until he saw them land safely, way up the cliffs, near the top. The two waved to him, signaling that they were all right. They would radio for help now, he knew.

"The Navy has a forward emergency station on the far side of the mountains," he told Tanya as they landed high on the steep mountainside. "I think I should fly us out to it."

"Leave? Now?" Tanya shook her head violently. "No!"

"Tanya, we've got no supplies. If we stay, we're asking for trouble."

"We've come this far, Archangel," she begged. "The very least we can do is have a look around. Can we—please?"

Archangel hesitated, frowning. It would be dark soon—and in this neighborhood, he remembered, it got real dark real fast. He guessed they would have to find shelter for the night in any case. There was no way he could fly them all the way out before nightfall.

And as he recalled, most of the *nasty* inhabitants of the Savage Land lived lower down, in the jungle. These highlands were pretty barren. They shouldn't be too dangerous.

"All right," he said, getting a huge sigh of relief and a grateful kiss on the cheek from Tanya. "You stay here and find us some shelter. We'll leave first thing in the morning."

"But what about you?" Tanya asked.

"I'm going back up there and scout around while it's still light," he told her. "I'll be back in a few minutes."

As it happened, he was back even sooner than that. "Tanya—I've found something!" he shouted as he alighted near where she was building a fire. "Here, let me show you."

He took her in his arms, and in an instant they were airborne, soaring gracefully on the updrafts, over peaks and canyons, until...

"Look, Tanya!"

She turned her head and gasped at what she saw. Almost completely filling the valley below stood the ruins of a futuristic city! Its great shattered dome towered above one of the natural geothermal pits that helped preserve the Savage Land's prehistoric environment.

"Magneto's citadel was here," Archangel told her as he landed on some rock debris overlooking the valley. Surveying the wreckage, he added, "One thing about the X-Men—you can generally tell where they've been."

"It's strangely...beautiful," Tanya said. "And so huge! We could wander through that place for years, and still only see a fraction of it!"

"This is an evil place, Tanya," Archangel told her. "This city was Magneto's base. From here he almost destroyed the Savage Land. Even now I can still sense the evil—"

Archangel broke off, turning around with a gasp. Tanya turned around, too, and what she saw made her scream in sheer terror.

They were surrounded by savage warriors, armed with some very sharp spears! Archangel and Tanya hardly had time to duck before the spears came hurtling at them.

Archangel quickly took off to draw their fire away from Tanya. He recognized these creeps—they were the same warriors who had once served Magneto. He thought they would have given up their violent ways, now that their leader had abandoned them.

At least he could stay at a safe distance from their spears up here. Or could he?

Suddenly, Archangel found himself blindsided by warriors riding on pterodactyls. An air force! This complicated things.

Before he could fly Tanya to safety, he would have to get rid of these Bronze-Age Red Barons. *It shouldn't be too hard, though,* he thought. Sure, he was outnumbered, but he was a lot faster than guys on dinosaurs. He also had the benefit of bio-metallic feathers, which could project out of his wings at will to pierce even the hardest steel. If he could get close enough to one of these warriors, he might actually be able to emit the paralyzing chemical contained in his feathers—

"Wha-a-att?"

Archangel's world turned topsy-turvy inside his head, as the senses he depended on for survival all went haywire at once.

He tried to dodge the attack of the mounted warriors, only to end up flying straight into a war axe! He fell earthward and landed hard, his head bleeding, his ribs aching. They were closing in on him fast, surrounding him. He only hoped Tanya was okay...

She wasn't. When Archangel had taken off, the warriors left on the ground turned their attention to her. Now they had her backed up to the edge of the cliff. Looking over her shoulder and down, she saw a rushing river below—a *hundred feet* below!

There was nowhere to run. She did know how to swim—*if* she survived the fall. Trying to remember the diving lessons she'd taken years ago in summer camp, she turned her back to her attackers and took a flying leap.

She hit the water hard—a lot harder than she'd imagined—and for a split second, she blacked out. Luckily, before her lungs filled with water, she came to and managed to fight her way up to the surface.

As she blinked and gulped for air, Tanya took stock. The river didn't seem too rough, thankfully. Nothing was broken. Things could be worse.

Just then, a spear landed in the water only a few feet to her left. Then another fell—this one to her right. Soon spears were raining down all around her. Tanya held her breath and ducked underwater once again, letting the current carry her downstream.

Archangel tried to get up, but it wasn't easy. His sense of balance was gone, the attack of vertigo getting worse. He stumbled to his feet just in time to see a giant running at him, spear in one hand, war axe in the other. The guy had to be at least nine feet tall!

Archangel leaned out of harm's way. If he hadn't been so dizzy, he'd have made short work of the giant. As it was, the huge warrior simply thundered past, swinging his war axe overhead and yelling at the top of his lungs.

Then Archangel saw another mutant striding toward him. And this one had four enormous arms! Archangel barely had time to think before those four arms pounded him mercilessly into oblivion.

❖   ❖   ❖   ❖   ❖   ❖   ❖

A short time later, and far downriver, Tanya Anderssen struggled through the thick undergrowth. She hadn't stopped since she hit the water, forced to keep moving by constant patrols of pterodactyl riders. She knew she couldn't make it much further.

As she had swum away from the scene of the battle, she'd heard a victory cheer. That meant those warriors had probably captured Archangel. Or...killed him.

Why did I come here? she asked herself bitterly. Was she as mad, as driven—as cursed—as Sauron?

"No!" she told herself. "I can't give up! Warren Worthington may still be alive. If I can find Ka-zar, lord of the Savage Land, he might be able to rescue Archangel...or at least avenge him."

Suddenly, there was a loud noise—the sound of huge trees snapping like twigs. And it was getting closer with every second.

"What is it?" she gasped. The answer rose up before her eyes, to its full, horrible height. She found herself gazing up into the hungry eyes of...

A *Tyrannosaurus rex!*

CHAPTER TWO

....

Primal Origins

Tyrannosaurus rex—"King of the tyrant lizards." A meat-eater with an enormous appetite. Though comparatively stupid, it kills with ease. *T. rex* is absolute monarch of its primordial domain.

Tanya Anderssen's knowledge of the dinosaur flashed before her, as if in a paragraph from an old encyclopedia. But all her knowledge could not help her now.

She was too scared to move or feel. Certain she was about to die, she prayed it wouldn't hurt too much.

And then, a loud warrior's yell and a

rumbling roar came from the undergrowth to Tanya's right. Both she and the tyrannosaur turned to see a blond warrior and a saber-toothed tiger racing toward them.

"Ka-zar! Zabu!" Tanya cried, recognizing the warrior as the lord of the Savage Land and the tiger as his ever-faithful companion.

"Do not be afraid!" Ka-zar shouted to her as he leapt onto the tyrannosaur. "Tonight, the lizard goes hungry!"

The dinosaur snapped at him with its jaws, but Ka-zar was too quick for it. In an instant, he was straddling the giant beast's head, out of range of both its claws and its teeth.

Meanwhile, Zabu slashed at the reptile's chest. "Warriors!" Ka-zar shouted at the top of his lungs. "Don't just stand there!"

"Warriors, attack!" came a cry from the bushes, and out rushed twenty or more eager fighters, spears in hand.

They're going to save me! Tanya thought, daring to hope again. Everything was going to be all rig—"Whugnnh!"

The huge beast's long tail whipped by, slamming straight into her head. Stars danced in her mind. She knew she was lying on the

ground, yet she still seemed to be falling, tumbling helplessly through space and time.

And then, all was blackness.

Archangel awoke with a headache beyond all comprehension. He needed an aspirin in the worst way. He opened his eyes to get one, only to find that his hands and body were bound to an upright basalt slab. He was in a large room, in the center of which loomed an enormous apparatus. One section of the machine was shaped like a huge telescope—and it was aimed straight at him!

Where am I? he wondered, trying to focus his eyes on the group that now surrounded him. The giant was there, as was the four-armed mutant who had knocked him unconscious. With them was a large, froglike monstrosity and a slim, green-haired woman whose face radiated evil.

At the controls of the machine sat a very strange-looking person. While his body was that of a child, his head was enormous and balding! His eyes shone with a sadistic wicked-ness. This mutant seemed to be the leader.

As Archangel's vision and his memory of

the fight both came back into focus, the tiny leader noticed him. "You're awake? Incredible! Barbarus's beating would have crushed a dozen ordinary men!" he exclaimed, eyes wide with admiration. "Welcome, human, to the citadel of our creator, Magneto."

Archangel's mind was a ball of fuzz. "I'm afraid we haven't been properly introduced."

"Of course," the little mutant said. "Forgive me. I am called Brainchild. I am master here. Blind Gaza, the giant, and four-armed Barbarus you have already met. My emerald-skinned comrade is Amphibius; the young lady, Vertigo. We are mutants. And soon we will be rulers of the Savage Land."

Archangel shifted subtly, trying to get his hands free. No dice. His captors certainly weren't taking any chances with him. And he definitely did not like the looks of that machine, either. But his head was pounding so hard, and his mind was so fuzzy...

Archangel knew he could break free using his bio-metallic wings, but he needed to stall for time, to get his strength back.

"What is this thing you've got pointed at me?" he asked.

Brainchild flashed him a sickening smile. "This device was used by Magneto to evolve us from simple swamp creatures into our present, superpowered forms. When the X-Men defeated Magneto, it was destroyed."

"It sure looks like it's in good shape now," Archangel said offhandedly, trying to mask his thoughts. He had to gain a few more minutes until he could figure out a way to get free.

"Yes, I've repaired it," Brainchild said, patting the machine's metal side proudly. "And I've added some interesting...modifications, too. Now, in addition to performing its original function of evolving an animal into a higher form of itself, it can also return any living being to its primitive beginnings. We had originally planned to test our device on Ka-zar—but now that *you* are here, Archangel, the honor will be *yours!*"

And that, Archangel thought, *is my cue.* He had used the last few moments well, employing the invincible strength of his bio-metallic wings to crack the steel bonds that held him and using his agility to wriggle loose. "Sorry, big brain," he said as he yanked his arms and legs free, "but flawed though I may be, I like myself just the way I am!"

"Vertigo!" Brainchild screamed, ducking behind the machine. "Deal with him!"

The green-haired woman faced Archangel. She extended her arms and a sickening wave of dizziness cascaded over him.

"Nooo!" He tried to resist, but he couldn't. The harder he fought the disorienting effects of Vertigo's power, the faster his world seemed to spin in circles.

But still he struggled mightily in a desperate attempt to break free—an attempt that was doomed to failure from the moment Brainchild activated the transformer.

As the moments slid by, Archangel sank back against the upright slab. It was getting more and more difficult to think. Sentences drifted out of reach, then words, leaving him only primal feelings—rage, pain, fear, hatred.

As simply and easily as an onion is stripped of its skin, so was Archangel stripped of his humanity. He felt himself drowning in an oily, black whirlpool within his mind. A terrible, terrifying scream followed him down into the darkness as he was pulled inexorably under.

At the last instant, with his last rational

thought, he realized that the scream was *his*.

The dinosaur was chasing Tanya, gaining ground with each earth-shaking step. In a matter of seconds, it would swallow her alive. She could feel its hot breath on her neck...

Tanya awoke screaming. A man was leaning down by her side, his face next to hers. It was his breath she had felt in her dream! She grabbed for him reflexively as her screams turned to anguished sobs, clinging to him with such desperation that her nails drew blood.

The man didn't seem to mind. "It's all right, Tanya," he murmured in her ear. "You're safe now. Nothing can hurt you. You're among friends. It's all right. It's all right."

"I...that voice..." Tanya gasped. "I know that voice!"

"You should know the face, too—though I admit I was relatively clean-shaven when you last saw me." He held her out at arm's length so she could get a good look at him. "Hello, Tanya."

"*Karl!* Oh, my darling, my love!"

She'd been so afraid that he had forgotten her or found someone else to care for. Not surprisingly, Lykos had felt the same fears. But with their first kiss both of them realized that their love was as strong as ever.

That evening, as she wolfed down a meal of fresh tyrannosaur steak, Tanya told her story to Karl, Ka-zar, and the latter's warriors—one hundred or so specially trained fighters, gathered from all the tribes of the Savage Land.

And then it was time for Ka-zar to tell Tanya of *his* mission. "Our goal is the ruined citadel where you and your friend were attacked. Its construction was ordered by Magneto. He meant to use it as a base from which to conquer the Savage Land.

"With the aid of the X-Men," he continued, "we ended Magneto's reign of terror. He fled, and his legions were dispersed, their power annihilated. Or so we thought.

"Lately, though, we've heard rumors of a resurgence of the evil army, this time led by a group of superpowered mutants created—well, evolved, really—years ago by Magneto. Now we are determined to find out what is going on—and nip the problem in the bud."

Karl Lykos put a hand on Ka-zar's arm.

"That, my friend, is beginning to look—"

He quickly whirled around as a snapping of bushes alerted them to movement around their camp's perimeter. "Ka-zar!" Lykos whispered, pointing. "Look at the thorn barrier!"

"Warriors, to arms!" Ka-zar shouted, leaping to his feet. "We are under attack!"

The thorn barrier parted, and a huge triceratops charged at them, followed by dozens of warriors—the same ones Tanya had encountered on the cliff with Archangel!

"They're hitting us from all sides!" Lykos shouted. Then he yelled in pain. "Aarrgh!"

"Karl!" Tanya gasped in horror as a birdlike creature with gigantic talons and murder in its eyes swiped at Lykos.

It looked like a giant bird, Tanya thought, as she gazed up at its silhouette in the darkness.

"Oh, no!" Tanya cried out. "Those scraps of costume—it can't be, but—but it *is*— Archangel!"

Archangel's cry was as inhuman as his appearance, as he dove once more toward the camp, scattering Ka-zar's fighters with his powerful wings. His beak and razor-sharp claws slashed in all directions at once.

Archangel had been transformed into a demonic creature, possessed by a berserker rage that could only be sated with blood.

Obeying an urge as old as life itself, Archangel, now reduced to his primordial self, dove down, grasped with his talons, then soared skyward with his captive—Tanya Anderssen.

CHAPTER THREE

....

A Monster Reborn

Unexpectedly deprived of its superpowered ally, the evil assault force was soon routed by Ka-zar's small but skilled band of fighters.

"Cowards!" Lykos shouted after the fleeing warriors. "Blood has been spilled this night—lives taken—and you have stolen the person in this world who is most precious to me! You *will* answer for this in kind!"

"I'm sure they're suitably impressed," Ka-zar said bitterly. "How badly were we hurt?"

"Eleven dead, nineteen wounded—and most of those will die by morning. Those butchers dipped their blades in poison!"

Thirty out of a hundred...a heavy toll. The captain of Ka-zar's elite force now stepped forward. "Ka-zar," he said, "we cannot continue without more men. I would be leading my warriors to slaughter."

"Ka-zar," Lykos broke in, "we can't afford to wait. Those savages took my Tanya!"

"I know, Karl," Ka-zar replied. "I saw."

"I hear a bitterness in your voice," the captain said to Ka-zar.

"It's anger and frustration," Ka-zar explained. "If we had access to a hospital, our fighters might at least have a chance at survival. I'm sorry. I love the Savage Land—but so much of the suffering you accept as the natural order of things seems to me so tragic, so...unnecessary."

"What's that on your knife, Ka-zar?" Lykos asked him.

"A piece of cloth," Ka-zar said, holding it up. "It's part of Archangel's costume."

"Was the monstrosity we fought...him?" Lykos asked, incredulous. "What fiend could have done that to him?"

"I don't know," Ka-zar said softly. "But it's time to find out."

Leaving the captain and the remainder of the warriors behind to nurse the wounded and bury the dead, Ka-zar, Zabu the tiger, and Lykos started immediately for the citadel.

As they approached the ruined city, the frequency and size of enemy patrols increased. Zabu and Lykos were more than ready to fight, but Ka-zar restrained them. Against such considerable odds, Ka-zar knew, they dared not tip their hand.

Meanwhile, in Brainchild's laboratory, Tanya awoke to find herself chained to an upright slab—the same slab that had earlier held the ill-fated Archangel.

"Good morning, Ms. Anderssen," a tiny mutant with an enormous head greeted her. "I trust you had a pleasant night's sleep."

"Who—who are you?" Tanya demanded. "What have you done to Archangel?"

"Fascinating," the little mutant observed. "You're obviously terrified, but still attempting to master your fear. I applaud your courage. I am Brainchild. My associates and I are mutants. Our intention is to conquer the Savage Land."

Tanya looked across the room at the collection of evil-looking mutants, which now included the monster that had once been her friend Archangel. In the same glance, she noticed the machine pointing straight at her.

"I'm very curious to see what this genetic transformer does to an ordinary human," said Brainchild, smiling. "You, Ms. Anderssen, will be my guinea pig."

"The devil she will, Brainchild!" Lykos's voice rang out as he, Ka-zar, and Zabu raced into the chamber, weapons at the ready.

"Karl! Oh, thank heavens!" Tanya cried.

"So much for the element of surprise," Ka-zar shouted as he swung his powerful fists into Amphibius, sending the froglike mutant flying. To his satisfaction, he saw that Lykos and Zabu had already succeeded in felling the giant Gaza. He turned to Lykos. "Move hard and fast, Karl, before they can activate that bloody machine!"

But his order came seconds too late. Chuckling, Brainchild pressed a switch, and raw energy turned Tanya's body to living fire. Image by image, memory by memory, Tanya felt her mind being stripped away.

"*Tanya!*" Lykos screamed in horror.

"Don't stand there, man! Charge!" Ka-zar shouted to him. "Don't give them a chance to react!"

"There's an easier way. Either Brainchild returns Tanya to normal—*now*—or I'll blow his brains out!"

Brainchild leveled a smug look at Lykos. "I assure you," he said, "your threat has me quaking in my boots. Vertigo! They're yours!"

The green-haired woman fixed them with her eyes, concentrating...and Karl Lykos's world turned upside down, inside out.

But even as all his physical senses came unglued, he managed to shoot a single ray from his energy blaster. Amazingly, it hit its target, knocking Vertigo unconscious.

As Vertigo fell, so did Lykos—completely disoriented by her psychic attack. Zabu sprang into action in his place, only to be met—and stopped in his tracks—by four-armed Barbarus.

"Ho, long-tooth!" the Neanderthal-faced mutant snarled. "Long have I awaited a chance to match my brute strength against yours!"

"Sorry, Charlie," Ka-zar interrupted with a wicked smash to Barbarus's face, "but anyone who hits my cat has to answer to *me!*"

Archangel now dove eagerly into the fray, slashing at Ka-zar's chest and forehead, drawing blood everywhere, grabbing Ka-zar fast in his talons. His grip tightened...

Ka-zar yelled in pain.

Barbarus now shook his head and lifted himself off the floor. "Many thanks, winged one," he said to Archangel. "While you hold the 'lord of the Savage Land' helpless, my four arms will quickly beat him to a pulp!"

But Barbarus had not reckoned with Karl Lykos, who had now recovered from his dizziness. Just as the four-armed monster prepared to strike, Lykos came rushing forward, knocking Barbarus off his feet, and sending him smashing right into the genetic transformer!

Sparks flew from the machine. It began to sizzle. Then it burst into flame and exploded, crumbling into a pile of rubble that covered Brainchild and his entire team of mutants!

Brainchild now came crawling out from underneath the wreckage. "The transformer— destroyed!" he cried.

But then his expression changed, and a sly smile came over his face. "Hah!" he laughed.

"Imbecile! You may have defeated me, but in the process you've cursed your friends! Without the transformer, they can never be restored to normal! Only *I* can reconstruct the device—and no power on earth can make me do it!"

Lykos felt a wave of sickness rise inside him. He turned and went over to the slab where Tanya lay—only it wasn't Tanya anymore. Although she wore the same clothes, Tanya was no longer human—she had become some sort of prehistoric creature!

She'd been devolved, Lykos knew. And he also knew that, without the transformer, she could never be cured. *Unless...*

He thought quickly. This transformer created primordial beings by injecting people with excess energy. He absorbed energy to live. If he drained that energy from Tanya, he might be able to return her to normal!

But there was a terrible risk. Small doses of energy could not harm him. But a large one might well alter him so drastically that he would transform into his evil self, Sauron!

"I can see no other solution," he whispered to himself. "If this gamble pays off, I can cure Tanya *and* Archangel."

So saying, he began to drain Tanya's energy. He had to be careful. The more power he took, the more he would crave. His human self must remain...in...control!

Tanya glowed as brightly as a newborn star, and when the glow faded—as abruptly as it had begun—she was her old self again!

Lykos now bent over Archangel, repeating the process.

Tanya looked up, still dazed by her ordeal. Her expression quickly turned from relief to horror at the sight before her.

"Ka-zar, it's Karl!" she shouted. "Stop him—before it's too late!"

"Witless woman," croaked a horrible voice, "it is already too late!"

That voice—it came from Karl Lykos! He now stood up and turned to face her. Archangel lay on the ground beneath him, turning human before her eyes—while the man she loved, Karl Lykos, was transformed into—a monster: half man, half pteranodon!

"Behold!" it croaked, its voice reverberating off the laboratory walls. "Behold the rebirth of—*Sauron!*"

CHAPTER FOUR

Enter the X-Men

"Look on me, humans, and despair!" Sauron shrieked hideously. "Never have I felt imbued with such invincible strength. Pathetic Karl Lykos is gone forever! Only Sauron remains!"

Like the others in the room, Ka-zar stared in silent horror at the winged fiend.

But Ka-zar also noticed that Sauron looked and sounded a bit shaky. The Sauron side of Karl Lykos's personality must not yet be fully dominant, he realized. If that was true, it meant he was still vulnerable. If they could take him on right now...

"You've been beaten before, bird-beak," he

called out impulsively, "and *cured!*"

But Sauron was too crafty to fall for Ka-zar's trick. The scheming dinosaur-man knew that Ka-zar wanted to lure him into a fight before he was strong enough to win. Instead, he took off, hovering over the broken dome that had once served as the lab's ceiling.

"Once, savage," Sauron called down to Ka-zar, "I would have crushed your bones to powder for such an insult. But now I am older and wiser. I know what you are planning and, consequently, will deny you even the opportunity of capturing me!"

The dinosaur-man called out a warning before he departed, soaring off into the mists.

"Mark me, Ka-zar," he croaked, "there is war between us! It will be as fierce and bloody as this land I was born to rule—and it can have but one ending. First I will take your wretched life—and then your soul!"

A few days later, a party of three arrived at the American research/rescue station just outside the Savage Land.

"I guess this is good-bye," Archangel said to the other two. "I wish I could stay, Ka-zar."

"I know, Archangel," Ka-zar replied. "But you need proper medical attention. I can't allow you to stay here.

"The good news is that my warriors scattered Brainchild's army," Ka-zar went on. "The bad news is that those blasted mutants escaped in the confusion. It will take time for them to regroup, however. It will take even more time for Sauron to mold them all into his army of conquest. I can use that grace period to recruit more soldiers to our cause. By the time I return, we should be ready for him."

"As for my decision to stay," Tanya added, "I've found the man I love. And that's far more important right now than my health. I won't rest—I can't—until Karl is cured, once and for all."

"You guys don't have to face Sauron alone," Archangel said. "He's as much the X-Men's responsibility as yours. Once I reach the main American base, I'll contact the X-Men at Xavier's School for Gifted Youngsters, and request their immediate presence in the Savage Land." He paused. "If you'll have us."

"The X-Men are always welcome in my domain," Ka-zar told him.

"Then it's settled," Archangel said, shaking Ka-zar's hand before boarding the helicopter that would take him to the main American base, where the hospital was located.

"Should I have left well enough alone?" Tanya asked, half to herself as the chopper lifted off. "Karl would still be himself, and a good, decent man would have been spared a horror that may scar him for the rest of his life. Not to mention the damage that will be inflicted upon the Savage Land. Is it really worth all this suffering?"

"Only you can answer that, Tanya," Ka-zar told her. "But remember, you stay here out of love—and Karl sacrificed himself out of love. You know…there are worse motivations."

Two hours earlier, and half a world away, it had been summer. Now, four members of the uncanny X-Men were wishing they were back home, enjoying the warmth of the season, rather than flying into the heart of the nastiest Antarctic blizzard any of them had ever seen.

Kurt Wagner, code-named Nightcrawler, was at the controls of the Blackbird, the X-Men's specially designed stratojet. "The further we go, Ororo," he said, addressing Storm by her birth name, "the rougher things become. Do you want me to turn around and wait somewhere for better weather?"

Storm shook her head, holding up the telegram they'd received back at headquarters. "According to this message, Archangel's situation is serious. Let us go on. I think the Blackbird can stand the strain."

"Yeah, but can we?" asked Wolverine, otherwise known as Logan.

"I know Cyclops would undoubtedly prove a better pilot," Nightcrawler replied, "but unfortunately, he is ill and had to stay behind. So you'll have to settle for me...unless you'd rather climb out and walk the rest of the way!"

"Relax!" Storm ordered. "I have been examining this blizzard since we first encountered it. I think I have learned enough to be able to moderate its effect on us."

But as Storm released her safety harness, a patch of turbulence sent her reeling into the arms of the husky Peter Rasputin, code-named Colossus.

"Thank you for catching me, Peter," Storm said. "I am all right. Let me up, please."

"As you wish, Ororo," Colossus replied, smiling.

"Any way I can help, darlin'?" Wolverine asked. "Just sittin' here, doin' nothin', is drivin' me buggy."

"*Wunderbar,*" interjected Nightcrawler in his native German. "The Blackbird's hit a patch of quiet air. Make your play, Ororo—quickly!"

She was named Ororo—Beautiful Wind-rider. As a child, she had watched her beloved parents killed before her eyes. In order to survive, she became a thief, and later, on the East African plain, a goddess to grateful tribes. Now, as a member of the X-Men, she reached out with her mind, becoming one with the tempest raging about the sleek skycraft. What her fellow X-Men saw as wind and snow, hail and sleet, Ororo perceived as patterns of energy.

Gently, she molded those awesome primal forces to her will, creating a bubble of clear, calm air around the Blackbird and guiding the stratojet safely to its destination. Soon the landing pad was in sight.

"The blizzard's fouling up our instruments," Nightcrawler said. "I'll have to make a visual, manual approach. Don't fail us now, Ororo! One stiff gust of wind, or a sudden downdraft, could splatter us all over the mountainside."

"I am...well aware of that, Nightcrawler!" Storm replied, panting with the effort she was exerting. *There is something...unusual about this tempest,* she thought to herself. It resisted her, as if it had a mind and will of its own. The strain was terrible. But she had to—she would—prevail!

The Blackbird's engines were drowned out by the ominous howl of the gale. But miraculously, in the teeth of the wind and snow and ice, Nightcrawler executed the smoothest of touchdowns.

"Okay, troops," Wolverine said happily. He stood up to stretch his legs. "We're where we're supposed ta be. What happens next?"

As if in answer to his question, the platform they'd landed on began descending through a chute inside the glacier! They went down, down, and down...until they reached a military base, buried one hundred meters beneath the surface!

Just then, Archangel emerged from a door-way and came forward to greet his friends.

"Archangel!" Storm said. "We came as quickly as we could!"

At that point, a uniformed man emerged from behind Archangel. "I'm Colonel Cath-cart," he said, shaking hands all around. "Welcome to Deep Ice Station Alpha. If you'll follow me to the briefing room..."

He led them along a bridgeway to the main base. "This is one of a half-dozen such installa-tions," Cathcart informed them, "scattered around the periphery of the Savage Land. In terms of natural resources, the Savage Land is blessed beyond imagining. Unfortunately, that bounty could easily prove too great a tempta-tion for some freebooting entrepreneur or country to resist.

"With that in mind, these bases were established to protect and study the Land, to keep its wealth in trust for future generations." So saying, Colonel Cathcart led the X-Men into the briefing room.

As they made themselves comfortable, Storm realized that she still felt uneasy. Her powers lent her a certain empathy with the earth, and she could tell that some unnatural force was affecting the workings of nature. If that force was allowed to grow unchecked, she feared, the results could be devastating.

"In your message, Archangel," she said, "you referred to a threat."

"I did indeed," Archangel answered. "Potentially, it's one of the worst we've ever faced." And then he told them of his and Tanya's adventures.

"...and Lykos absorbed the energy used to degenerate us," he finished. "He returned Tanya and me to normal. But in the process, he was transformed once more into his evil persona: Sauron!"

The X-Men were stunned into silence. But suddenly, that silence was broken by a violent rumbling and shaking!

"The ceiling is buckling!" Nightcrawler shouted. *"Earthquake!"*

CHAPTER FIVE

Victory...
and Defeat

On the surface of the Savage Land, the ancient peaks of the Eternity Mountains shuddered, and a basso rumble filled the air as the earth tremors triggered a series of massive avalanches. Below, in the heart of the glacier, the situation was far worse.

"Colossus!" Storm cried out. "Turn to armor! Use your strength to keep the ceiling from falling!"

In a burst of energy, the young Russian mutant transformed himself to superstrong, nigh-invulnerable organic steel. He braced himself and pressed his hands against the sagging ceiling, bearing it up.

"You caught it!" Storm shouted. "But that must weigh tons, Colossus—can you hold it?"

"Easily, Storm! Wolverine, give me a hand. We will use some I-beams to brace the ceiling and prevent further collapse." The two X-Men worked quickly together.

And then the quake was over. The emergency lights came on, and they could see again.

"This place is a mess!" Wolverine groaned, surveying the wreckage of the base. "C'mon, heroes—we got a lot o' work to do." Calling out to anyone within earshot, he added, "Sing out if you're trapped an' we'll cut ya free!"

Storm did her part, along with the others. This earthquake, she realized, was no more natural than the blizzard had been. She would have sensed the stress in the fabric of the earth if natural forces had been responsible. But she had felt nothing. Some power, some being, had deliberately triggered the shock.

Meanwhile, Nightcrawler had heard a faint tapping from the far side of a wall of debris. Dimly seeing movement through a gap in the wreckage, he teleported to the other side, reached the neighboring chamber, and returned with a wounded soldier.

A temporary hospital was established on a lower level of the base, and the X-Men painstakingly carried the wounded there, one by one.

"This isn't the first such freak quake we've experienced," Colonel Cathcart told the X-Men as they finished their task. "Each time, the epicenter has been near a Deep Ice station. Our defenses are being tested, Storm—by whom and for what purpose, I don't know. I've sent patrols to try to contact Ka-zar. They have all disappeared without a trace."

Later, after the base had been returned to a semblance of normalcy, Cathcart led the X-Men to a cave which served as the main surface entrance to the Savage Land.

"I wish there were more of you," he said. "If you fail, the great powers will have no choice but to use military force against Sauron. That would mean the end of the Savage Land—and it might also mean dire consequences for the earth itself!" With those ominous words, he took his leave of them.

Alone together, the X-Men stared down

the dark tunnel. "Five of us, against who knows what," Storm said. "One could wish for better odds."

"Wind's blowin' up-tunnel from the Savage Land," Wolverine said, sniffing. "I mark no hostile scents. The exit's clear."

"Good, Wolverine," Storm said. "Archangel, you take the point. Scout as far as the encampment of Ka-zar's elite guard. We'll stay in touch using our micro-transceivers."

Archangel flew ahead, and the rest of the X-Men proceeded slowly into the cave. They emerged on the other side a few hours later, wearier for the long walk.

But any fatigue was forgotten at their first sight of the Savage Land. Each X-Man instinctively felt the absolute power and majesty of this great land.

"This is my kinda world, people," Wolverine said, taking a deep breath. "I hope it never changes."

"If this place turns you on, runt, you're more than welcome to it."

They all looked up to see Archangel hovering in the sky above. "Storm," he said ominously, "we've got trouble!"

"There was no need to report in person, Archangel," Storm said. "Why didn't you use your radio?"

Archangel looked at them darkly. "What I found isn't the sort of thing a person can talk about." So saying, he grabbed Colossus and took off again. Storm flew behind, Wolverine and Nightcrawler dangling from her hands.

"*Tovarisch,* what is the matter?" Colossus asked Archangel. "What did you find?"

"You'll see...There it is—the camp of Ka-zar's elite guard. Or at least, it *was.*"

The X-Men stared down in the direction indicated by Archangel. A terrible sight greeted them. The camp had been burned to the ground, its log houses torched. In the middle of the clearing, three huge crosses had been erected. And to each of those crosses was bound one of Ka-zar's warriors, dead!

"A warning, obviously," Archangel said. "To remind all Ka-zar's people of the price of resistance." He gritted his teeth and added, "It's hard to believe one human being could do this to another."

Wolverine's eyes blazed with fury. "Our capacity to kill is as infinite as our capacity to love. But when I kill, it's out of necessity, or passion. This is murder as an act of policy—cold-blooded and merciless. You may not believe me, but there's a difference."

Sniffing, Wolverine turned to Nightcrawler. "I mark a scent," he whispered. "Near the tree line—say, forty meters bearing two o'clock relative. Check it out—but watch yourself. This sucker feels big."

"On my way, Logan," Nightcrawler replied with a quick nod. He disappeared in an instant, and reappeared not a second later behind a giant of a man. *This has to be the blind mutant, Gaza,* he thought, remembering the descriptions Archangel had given them. With one quick leap, he jumped onto the giant's back and wrapped an arm around his neck, trying to throw him to the ground.

But Gaza was stronger than Nightcrawler had realized. The giant threw the lithe X-Man off his back as if he were a kitten. Wheeling around, Gaza raised his staff to strike.

"You'll not hold me!" he raged.

The staff swung around—and missed, as Nightcrawler teleported out of its reach just in time! But Gaza, in a surprise move, turned back around and raced for the clearing—straight toward Wolverine.

The giant's speed was phenomenal. Wolverine was rarely caught off guard, but this time, Gaza's staff had cracked into his skull before he even knew what hit him.

Fortunately, Storm prevented any further damage by aiming a blast of wind at Gaza, sending him sprawling. In another moment, the battle was over. Colossus had put the giant in a stranglehold.

Archangel approached the fallen Gaza. "I said I'd return, Gaza, and I have," he said.

Gaza stared back at him with his blind eyes. Archangel knew that the giant was using his mutant psychic powers to "see" him. "Aye, winged one, and I and my comrades pledged to slay you if you did—and we shall yet!"

As if on command, Vertigo stepped out from behind the trees, spreading her arms out toward the X-Men! Her power ripped into their minds, sending their world spinning inside out, upside down. They staggered and fell, unable to tell reality from illusion.

In their debilitated state, the X-Men became easy prey for Amphibius and Barbarus,

who now emerged from their cover in the trees. But the X-Men weren't finished yet.

Nightcrawler, on his knees, tried to keep his head from spinning. It wasn't easy. He kept losing his balance. But he had learned to cope with that dizzy sensation in his youth, during his days with the circus, when he'd been trained on the trapeze and the high wire. He focused his concentration and finally mastered his senses.

Still, he knew he would not be able to hold out long against this force that was hammering at his consciousness. He had to act fast.

The vertigo effect was what Archangel had reported suffering from during his first encounter with these evil mutants. *It seems to be coming from that woman over there,* he thought.

Nightcrawler couldn't reach her on foot— there was too much chance of being spotted—and he was too woozy to teleport. Instead, he sent a stone!

The projectile hit Vertigo smack in the temple. She fell to the ground in a heap, unconscious. Freed from her spell, the X-Men rose to their feet as the other evil mutants began to back away, fear chilling their bones at the loss of their comrade.

"We're obliged, elf," Wolverine told Nightcrawler.

Then he turned his attention to the cowering group of mutants. "I figure I speak for my buddies here. We don't like anyone messin' with our minds. An' we don't have words to tell you how we feel about what was done to this encampment and its people. So we intend to let our actions speak for us!"

The second round of the battle was as furious as the first. And the results were decisively in the X-Men's favor.

Watching the scene on a monitor from his laboratory in the citadel, Brainchild cried out, "My fellow mutants are being defeated!"

But a soothing voice from behind him said, "Be patient. Fear not. I will yet be triumphant."

"As you say, Sauron," Brainchild said with a little bow. "You are our master now."

Unaware of the sinister force watching them, the X-Men now began to interrogate their prisoners. It was the mutant Amphibius who proved the most informative.

"I...I will talk," the green-skinned mutant said. "But out of choice, not fear. Soon after Sauron was reborn, Ka-zar and his accursed saber-toothed tiger, Zabu, vanished from the Savage Land. Their disappearance—combined with our victory here over Ka-zar's elite guard—removed the only major obstacles to our conquest of the Savage Land.

"We mutants provided the power to smash any foe, and our backup reinforcements made our victories secure. And of course, Sauron provided us with the leadership that made it all possible. Under his direction, we have built a new citadel. It is impregnable, situated on an island in the center of one of the Great Central Lakes. If you want Sauron, seek him there. We will even show you the way."

Wolverine looked down at the prone Amphibius with a snarl. "You're bein' awfully cooperative, bub," he said suspiciously.

Amphibius smiled up at him, nervously flicking his tongue. "You were doomed, X-Men, the moment you set foot in Sauron's domain."

"Wanna bet?" Wolverine shot back. He

began to unsheathe his terrifying adamantium claws.

"Retract your claws, Wolverine!" Storm ordered. "We do not harm our prisoners—regardless of the provocation."

Grumbling, Wolverine reluctantly obeyed. And so, their captives in tow, the X-Men set off through the jungle. Before long, the hothouse atmosphere began to take its toll on them. Yet on...and on...and on they went, for what seemed like an eternity.

Suddenly, it occurred to Storm that she should have summoned reinforcements, or at least sent word to Colonel Cathcart, before they set out for Sauron's citadel.

What is wrong with me? she wondered. She had settled this question hours ago—why was she still questioning her own decision?

"Tired, Windrider?" taunted Amphibius. "Perhaps you would like to rest. Untie me and I will help make that rest permanent."

The heat didn't seem to be getting to Amphibius at all, or to any of his fellow evil mutants, for that matter. They all seemed to be holding up just fine.

"Button it, froggy!" Wolverine growled. He

lashed out with his claws, but slashed only empty air as Amphibius hopped nimbly out of reach.

Impossible! Wolverine couldn't believe he'd missed the sucker! It was this heat...

"Pathetic little man!" Amphibius needled. "If you intend to hurt me, you'll have to do far better than that!"

And then, a shadow fell upon them all—a giant dark presence, entirely blocking out the sun. The X-Men looked up tiredly. From far above, a hideous squawking voice screeched out to them.

"Yield, X-Men! Whether you resist or not, the victory this day belongs to—*Sauron!*"

CHAPTER SIX

Broken Wills

Behind and above Sauron rode dozens of savage warriors on pterodactyls, all armed with spears. Sauron himself now swooped down low over the weakened X-Men.

"Confused, mutants?" he asked. "Unsure what to do or how to react? Then let my irresistible hypnotic gaze add immeasurably to your difficulties!"

His eyes caught theirs for only an instant, but that was enough to give the villain access to their most personal and primal terrors. To their horror, the X-Men found themselves— and their world—twisted beyond imagining into something hideous and incalculably evil.

It was a sensation Archangel knew only too

well. And it was more than he could bear. "No! Not again!" he screamed in fright. With a hasty flapping of wings, he took flight and disappeared off into the distance.

Laughing, Sauron followed. Storm tried to stop him, but her arms turned into snakes that strangled her. She knew it was illusion and fought it with all her strength—but in vain.

Meanwhile, Archangel glanced behind him to see Sauron closing in. The monster's hypnotic gaze hadn't affected him as badly as the others, he realized now. Perhaps because of all his previous exposures, he had developed a partial immunity.

Lost in thought, Archangel reacted almost too late as Sauron swooped at him, just missing one of his wings. Archangel had forgotten how agile Sauron was!

But from the X-Men's computer profile of Sauron, Archangel did know the monster's only weakness—cold! Freezing temperatures would chill the cold-blooded dinosaur-man, throwing him into an instant stupor—and eventually causing death! Remembering, he took off into the upper atmosphere, trying to lure Sauron after him.

"Clever boy, Archangel!" Sauron shouted, flying downward, away from the pursuit. "Did you hope to freeze me out? Hah! So long as I have your friends, I have nothing to fear from you!" So saying, Sauron headed back to his citadel.

Sauron is right, Archangel thought bitterly. The dinosaur-man had the upper hand as long as the X-Men remained his prisoners. But how had he taken them so easily? Just before Sauron's attack, he remembered, they had all been feeling out of it—tired and bored.

Suddenly, a strong blast of freezing wind knocked the breath out of him and sent him reeling. He'd accidentally flown into an Antarctic jet stream!

It was so cold! Before he knew it, his bio-metallic wings were coated with ice. Gravity began to reassert itself, and Archangel—like the famous Icarus of Greek mythology—tumbled from the sky.

The warmer air near the ground revived him somewhat. The ice began to melt off his wings and he beat them wildly—in a desperate attempt to pull out of his dive.

The effort was magnificent—but it was too

little, too late. There was an instant of crushing, unendurable pain—then oblivion.

Later, in the throne room of the new citadel, Sauron confronted his prisoners.

"Welcome, fools, to my fortress," he chuckled fiendishly. "Your stay will last a lifetime, and I am happy to say it will be far from pleasant. Indeed, the fate I have in store for you is as appropriate as it is horrible.

"X-Men, you have opposed me for the last time," he said, surveying his intended victims who knelt, shackled, before him.

With an effort, Wolverine lifted his head. "The war goes on, bub," he said defiantly.

"Perhaps, Wolverine," Sauron said, leaning forward, "but your part in it is over. Haven't you wondered how my forces were able to capture you all so easily? Your bonds are formidable—for humans—but with your vaunted mutant powers, you should have no trouble breaking free. Yet you haven't even tried!

"You see, I have created an energy field surrounding this citadel that saps the will of all who approach. My army is shielded from its effects. You are not. The closer you came, the weaker it made you. By the time I finally closed in for 'the kill,' as it were, you were virtually helpless."

Storm winced. An energy field! That explained her confusion, her lack of concentration! She'd known things had been going too smoothly—why hadn't she realized the danger sooner?

Sauron's evil henchmen led the shackled X-Men from the throne room to a nearby laboratory.

Before they knew it, the X-Men were strapped with bands of steel to upright basalt slabs. Pointing forbiddingly at them was a huge machine, very much like the one that had been destroyed just a few weeks before.

"This device is a mutant energy accelerator," Sauron informed the X-Men. As he had previously, Brainchild manned the controls while the other evil mutants stood by, watching with malicious grins on their faces.

"It is capable of evolving or degenerating a being. I believe that your friend Archangel has already experienced the fascinating effects of such a devolution. Now it is your turn. I intend to reduce you to a primitive state, making you little better than beasts. You know that I sustain myself by absorbing life energy. Draining that excess mutant energy from you—by periodically returning you to normal—will provide me with an inexhaustible supply of food. The will-destroyer should prevent any plans of escape during your brief periods of normalcy, before the accelerator returns you once more to prehistoric oblivion."

"*Monster!*" Colossus cried out. "By the White Wolf, if I were free—"

"But you are *not* free, Colossus," Sauron reminded him. "You will never be free again. In fact...Brainchild, begin with *him*."

The genius mutant complied, and a low hum filled the room—quickly to be drowned out by a scream of agony.

For a moment, it seemed that Colossus's armored body might shield him from the effects of the mutant energy accelerator ray.

Then, before his friends' disbelieving eyes, his features began to melt and re-form. He transformed inside and out, howling like a lost soul, as he was pitched headlong into darkness.

CHAPTER SEVEN

A Daring Plan

In another part of the Savage Land, Archangel discovered, much to his surprise, that he was very much alive.

"I can't believe it! It's a miracle!" he gasped, touching himself all over to make sure no bones were broken. "But—where am I? Whose camp is this?"

Archangel's vision kept going in and out of focus. He thought he saw a man standing in front of a lean-to—a giant of a man with long blond hair and a cheerful grin.

"How quickly they forget," the man said. "It's *my* camp, Archangel."

Archangel's vision cleared. "You—Ka-zar...? *Ka-zar!*"

"Welcome back to the land of the living, stranger," Ka-zar said, beaming down at him. A small dinosaur—the prize of his hunt—lay draped over his shoulders. By his side stood Zabu, panting from the chase.

"For a while there, Zabu and I thought you weren't going to make it."

"Pal, am I glad to see you!" Archangel said, rubbing the back of his head, where there was a bump the size of an orange. "Heck, I'm glad to see anyone! I was sure that I was a dead man. But my wings must have cut my speed enough so that the impact of the fall only knocked me out! How long have I been unconscious?"

"Hard to tell. The perpetual mist that shrouds the sun and stars above the Savage Land makes it difficult to tell time." Ka-zar laid his burden down and proceeded to cut it up into large chunks for their dinner.

"I'm afraid you've been out for a while, though," he continued. "You may feel fine now, but you were pretty far gone when we found you. In your dreams you kept shouting

out the names of the other X-Men."

After cutting two hunks for them, Ka-zar called, "Here, Zabu—dinner." Purring, the saber-tooth dragged away the rest of the dinosaur carcass to a corner of the clearing.

Archangel began filling Ka-zar in on everything that had happened to him since they'd parted at the American forward base.

Ka-zar listened, struck to the marrow. "I didn't know about my elite guard...or the capture of the X-Men," he whispered hoarsely. "I've been away. When I left, Sauron's threat seemed minimal, under control..."

"Well, it isn't anymore."

"I told Tanya Anderssen to stay with my elite guards," Ka-zar said, blinking back his pain. "I figured she would be safer there..."

"Did you go to summon more help, Ka-zar?" asked Archangel sympathetically.

"Yes. I went to Pangea, at the far frontier of the Savage Land, to recruit reinforcements for our small army. I knew Sauron would be back eventually—but so soon! I was only gone for a few weeks!"

"The same few weeks it took for Professor Xavier to round up the X-Men and send them down here to meet me," Archangel said. "And in those same few weeks, Sauron not only gained full strength but also rounded up the evil mutants, reorganized their army under his control, and built a new citadel!"

"Incredible!" Ka-zar breathed. "I knew his powers were formidable, but this—!"

"By the way," Archangel said, "we didn't find any female corpses at the encampment. Tanya could be a prisoner with the X-Men."

Ka-zar cast his eyes downward, ashamed at having lost Tanya. Archangel, seeing the look, said quickly, "Look, I could fly out to one of the new United Nations bases on the periphery of the Savage Land and request reinforcements..."

"I doubt we have the time," Ka-zar said, shaking his head. Holding out a hunk of dinosaur flesh for Archangel, he added, "Here—you'll think better on a full stomach."

"Thanks, but I prefer my meals cooked."

"Can't," Ka-zar replied, tossing the hunk of flesh Zabu's way. "Too much danger of a fire being spotted by Sauron's scouts.

"As you know, if Sauron absorbs the X-Men's mutant energy, he can increase his own power exponentially. By the time any assistance arrives, he might well be unbeatable."

He ate a few bites of dinosaur flesh, lost in thought. "How was Sauron able to defeat the X-Men?" he finally asked.

"I...don't know," Archangel replied. "Before he attacked, we were all feeling lousy— out of sorts, tired; it was an effort to think, much less act. By the time he struck, we'd lost our will to resist."

Suddenly, it all came clear to Archangel. "That must be it!" he said, snapping his fingers. "Sauron's evil mutants have built some kind of device to weaken the resolve of anyone who invades their leader's territory."

"But Sauron doesn't trust anyone," Ka-zar pointed out. "Which means he certainly wouldn't devise such a weapon unless he either controlled or powered it. He'd be too afraid of it being turned against him. So if someone were to lure him from his citadel, someone *else* might have a chance to sneak inside and free the prisoners."

"By 'someone,'" Archangel said quietly, "do you mean me?"

"You've got the wings."

"I can't. You don't understand! He's been in my mind, my soul—the thought of facing him a third time is almost more than I can bear. Ka-zar, I *can't* do it."

"Then our friends and this Land are doomed, flyboy—because I can't do it alone."

For a long time, Archangel was silent, his face showing his inner turmoil as fear raged against duty. Until, finally, a new resolution appeared in his features.

"Okay. I promise nothing...but I'll try."

At dawn the next morning, the two companions and Zabu stood on a ridge overlooking the Great Lake. Sauron's enormous citadel stood on an island in the middle of the lake, but it was barely visible through the morning mist.

"I don't feel any of the sensations I experienced last time," Archangel said. "Sauron's will-destroyer must be inactive."

Looking across to the hazy form of the citadel, he added, "That lake's pretty wide, Ka-zar, and brimming with aquatic carnivores. Are you determined to swim it?"

"As fast as I possibly can," Ka-zar answered

as he finished rigging up the large catapult they'd fashioned overnight. "Don't worry, though. I'll have Zabu to keep me company. Light our 'warhead,' flyboy, and let's get your part of the action started!"

Meanwhile, within the fortress, Sauron paced the length of the laboratory anxiously. "How much more time, Brainchild?" he demanded. "I hunger."

"Only a few more seconds, master," the tiny mutant with the huge head replied. He completed the final sequence of machine commands. "Behold! The final transformation begins!"

The four X-Men lay on their upright slabs before the mutant energy accelerator. The men were human. Storm, the team's leader, was human no longer. She was now what *Homo sapiens* had been on a lower rung on the evolutionary ladder: more than ape, but less than human.

Brainchild caressed his controls, eyes alight with anticipation. He delighted in the scientific ramifications of these human experiments. In fact, he would have liked to conduct more variations of the procedure on the help-less Storm.

A blinding white light reached to the very core of Storm's being. Then skin and bones began to melt and flow like wax as, step by agonizing step, she climbed the evolutionary ladder, following her friends and teammates back into never-ending nightmare.

"Sauron..." she gasped as she came to herself again. "There are not...words...to describe...you..."

"Your will is as matchless as your courage, my dear," Sauron mocked. "And neither shall avail you aught. Before you recover the full use of your powers, I will drain the mutant energy from your bodies. Then Brainchild's accelera-tor will once more return you all to a subhuman state. When you are almost totally unreasoning hominids, your threat to me will become nonexistent!"

But at that precise instant, a fireball crashed through the roof, smashing into the lab! Sirens sounded throughout the citadel.

"The alarm!" Brainchild exclaimed. "We are under attack! But who would dare?"

Fwhoom! Another explosion ignited a blaze

at the far end of the room.

And now, through the broken roof, they could discern a winged figure hovering in the sky above them...

"Archangel!" Sauron screeched in fury.

"That's right, ugly!" Archangel called down to his greatest enemy. "I'll make this offer once. I advise you to accept. Release the X-Men and your other prisoners, and surrender—or face the consequences!"

"The youth is demented!" Sauron gasped in astonishment. But slowly, his face regained a hideous composure. He moved toward Storm, grasping her head with his talons. "Is it not ironic that those whom Archangel seeks to save are providing me with the power to destroy him?"

Sauron drained the life energy from all four X-Men in quick succession. "Double the guard," he ordered his evil mutants. "This challenge could be a trick. Brainchild, degenerate the X-Men."

But as the genius mutant reprogrammed the accelerator, his gaze strayed once more to Storm, lolling unconscious on her slab.

Meanwhile, Sauron had flown up to greet

his challenger. "Do you miss your comrades so much, mutant," he asked, "that you have come to share their fate?"

Archangel wasted not a moment in his reply. "So long as a single X-Man remains free, monster, you haven't won!"

From his lookout spot on the shore, Ka-zar watched as Archangel turned and flew off with Sauron in hot pursuit.

"That's the spirit, flyboy," Ka-zar said under his breath. "Lead him as far away from the citadel as you can."

"*Rrrrr...*" Zabu growled.

"You got it, Zabu," Ka-zar said. "That's our cue to get wet!"

CHAPTER EIGHT

....

The X-Men Strike Back

Ka-zar hit the water and surfaced for air, thinking about Archangel. The winged mutant had known the odds—that he'd be outmatched from the start. Yet he was still giving it everything he had.

Deep in these reflections, Ka-zar failed to notice an object cutting a swift path through the water, coming closer with every second. Finally, he heard a rushing sound, and looked up to see a giant dinosaur swimming straight at him—with open jaws! Thinking quickly, Ka-zar twisted to one side.

The next time the aquatic beast lunged,

Ka-zar was ready. He grabbed hold of the dinosaur, wrapping an arm around its neck.

At this, the ghastly prehistoric beast reared its enormous head out of the water. Quickly, Ka-zar drew his knife. The dinosaur had only one vulnerable point. He had to hit it on the first try.

The knife struck swiftly—and the blow was fatal. As the gigantic beast screamed in its death agony, Ka-zar sighed with relief. "At least one thing has gone right today," he mumbled to himself. "Now I've just got to reach that citadel before Sauron returns."

He swam with everything in him for the island where the citadel stood. The beast was too busy dying to bother with him anymore, but its blood would attract other beasts and drive them into a killing frenzy. So the sooner he reached dry land again, the better.

Zabu—where was Zabu?

"I should have known," Ka-zar said, grinning as he looked up and saw the saber-tooth, already awaiting him on the island's shore. Ka-zar swam the few remaining yards and Zabu pulled him up with his gentle jaws. "You're letting me fight my own battles these days, huh? Your confidence in me is touching."

The saber-tooth began licking him affectionately. "Stop fussing now, I'm all right. Honest," Ka-zar said, chuckling.

"Not a sound, cat," he ordered as they moved stealthily through the undergrowth toward the citadel. "They'll be expecting trouble up there. We can't let 'em know we've arrived until we're ready." *And wherever you are, Archangel,* he thought to himself, *keep up the good work. Just buy me a little more time...*

Way up in the clouds, Archangel was going flat out, using every scrap of skill and experience to compensate for Sauron's superior power—and so far, he was holding his own, trading blow for blow.

They had almost reached the mountains that ringed and protected the Savage Land. Archangel knew that the key to defeating Sauron lay in forcing him out of the Savage Land's hothouse environment and into an Antarctic jet stream.

"Have you forgotten?" Sauron shouted, interrupting Archangel's thoughts. "I long ago took your measure—and found you wanting!"

And with that, Sauron leveled his amazing hypnotic gaze at Archangel.

"*Nooo!*" the X-Man screamed.

The last thing he felt before he lost consciousness was Sauron's talons grabbing him, carrying him back toward the citadel.

Meanwhile, in a secret chamber within the fortress, Brainchild was dishing out some extra torture to Storm. Her beauty, her spirit, and the fact that she was the leader of the despised X-Men singled her out as the focus of his sadistic attention.

Just as he was about to begin a particularly gruesome experiment, in burst Zabu and Ka-zar!

There was no time for Brainchild to alert the guards. Zabu's rush sent him hurtling smack into the stone wall. Brainchild fell to the floor, unconscious.

"Are you all right, Ororo?" Ka-zar asked, freeing Storm from the bonds that held her.

"Weak, but otherwise unharmed—thanks to your timely arrival," she replied.

"Rest yourself, then, while I deal with Brainchild," Ka-zar said, unsheathing his knife.

"Ka-zar, no!" Storm said, grabbing his knife arm. "You must not kill him!"

"You know that if our positions were reversed, he wouldn't hesitate an instant to kill *me*," Ka-zar said.

"But are we not supposed to represent a nobler ideal than he?" Storm asked.

"All right," Ka-zar said. "But I hope we don't live to regret it. Can you use your powers?"

"I...do not know," Storm said. "Sauron drained so much of my strength that I can barely walk. And the residual effects of his will-destroyer make it difficult for me to focus my concentration."

"I was afraid of that," Ka-zar said as he stopped in front of a small cell to gaze at its occupant. What he saw made him gape in dismay. "Dear God—I feared this most of all."

"Blessed Goddess!" Storm gasped. "Tanya Anderssen—degenerated! As I was!"

"*Hrrrrrar!*" roared Tanya, furiously reaching out for Ka-zar with her gnarled, hairy hands.

He dodged her grasp. "There isn't a glimmer of intelligence or recognition in her eyes," he said. "She's Tanya all right...yet no trace remains of her human self."

"The process can be reversed, Ka-zar," Storm assured him.

"I know," Ka-zar said grimly. "But seeing her like this, imagining what she's gone through..." He heaved a sigh. "I'm putting an end to Sauron and to his little mob of evil mutants once and for all."

"*Yeeeyarrrgh!*" The sudden sound issued from the far end of a long corridor.

"It's Nightcrawler!" Storm gasped. "They're using the accelerator on him!"

Swiftly, silently, the trio raced back through the fortress until they reached the laboratory. There they saw Gaza standing guard.

"Stay here, Ororo," Ka-zar whispered. "I'll handle this."

Storm had never seen Ka-zar so grim, nor felt so grim herself. This once, she wished she could set aside her oath never to take a life. For what was done to her, and her friends, she would gladly have torn the living heart from Sauron's breast with her bare hands!

By the time Ka-zar rendered Gaza sense-less, Nightcrawler's screams had become bestial howls that chilled Storm to the marrow. The other X-Men lay on their slabs near him—tossing and turning in their unnatural, tortured sleep.

Surrounding the accelerator were dozens of savage warriors acting as guards during Sauron's absence. Amphibius was working the controls of the machine.

Once upon a time, African tribes had called Storm a goddess. The description was not far off the mark—for her power was that of the primal elements of nature. At her summons, lightning flared star-bright around her, thunder boomed like a celestial cannon, and an irresistible wind swept Amphibius and the savage warriors helplessly away.

It was an awesome display, but not without cost. No sooner had she accomplished her momentous task than Storm fainted in Ka-zar's arms. "Ororo!" he cried.

"Ooohhhh…surprised myself that time," Storm groaned, coming to. "Didn't think…I had that much…strength left in me…I'll be fine, Ka-zar. Just need…few moments to catch my breath…"

Meanwhile, Zabu went over to where

Wolverine was strapped down and began licking his face.

"Huh? Whuzzat?" Wolverine asked, awakening from his trance. "Hiya, cat! Cripes, your tongue's like sandpaper—but pain's good... helps me...focus...thoughts. Storm, that side panel...localized will-destroyer..."

"I know, Wolverine," Storm said, shutting it off. "It keeps us quiet when Sauron isn't nearby. Brainchild boasted about it to me. There, it's off."

"Can't fault your timing, Storm," Ka-zar said, looking toward the far end of the room. As he spoke, dozens more of Sauron's soldiers appeared in the doorway. "We got company."

At Ka-zar's warning, Wolverine extended his unbreakable adamantium claws and strained against his bands. "These clamps— too strong! Someone cut me loose!"

"And be quick about it!" Ka-zar agreed, drawing his knife to face his onrushing attackers. "I could use some help!"

"Colossus!" Storm called to the awakening strongman. "Change to your armored form. Then you can break through with ease!"

Colossus blinked his eyes, fuzzy-headed.

"I...will try, Storm...but it is so hard to think...to concentrate..."

Gradually, though, a field of raw energy surrounded the young Russian, and flesh and blood became superstrong organic steel. In seconds, the steel clamps snapped like peanut brittle.

"I am free!" Colossus exulted, going over to release Wolverine. "And now, little comrade, so are you!"

"Much obliged, bub," Wolverine thanked him with a grin of anticipation. "How's about the pair of us start teachin' these lowlifes the error of their ways?"

CHAPTER NINE

Deep Freeze

Then the battle began, and it was fierce beyond description. The odds were stacked against the X-Men, and a lesser bunch might have given themselves up then and there. But the X-Men, side by side with Ka-zar and Zabu, fought valiantly on.

Meanwhile, Storm sat at the controls of the accelerator, trying to figure out how to operate the infernal machine. She was still too weak to effectively control her powers. If she tried to use them now, she knew, she would only do more harm than good.

But her mind was clear. She had to try to activate the sequence that would restore Nightcrawler to normal.

On one side of her, Colossus did battle with four-armed Barbarus. On her other, Wolverine was busy knocking Vertigo out of commission. And behind her, Ka-zar and Zabu were putting Sauron's soldiers to flight.

Meanwhile, the accelerator's low hum began to fill the chamber, a macabre counterpoint to Nightcrawler's howls of anguish.

Hastily, Storm punched in the final commands she hoped would re-evolve Nightcrawler. *Have I keyed in the correct pattern?* she wondered. A mistake could do Nightcrawler irreparable harm!

"That's the lot of 'em, Ka-zar!" Wolverine shouted as Vertigo fell to the ground, knocked senseless. "How's Nightcrawler? Is he okay?"

"See for yourself, Wolverine," Storm said. Nightcrawler, still strapped to his slab, was as still as stone. He looked as if he'd been through a living nightmare—but he was himself again.

"Not bad," Wolverine said, surveying the room where their foes lay defeated on the floor.

"Ours may be a hollow triumph, my friends," Storm put in, "so long as Sauron remains free."

"Storm!" The voice was Nightcrawler's. And there was an odd note in it, something Storm had rarely heard in Nightcrawler's voice—a note of fear. "All of you—*look!*"

They turned their gazes toward the hole in the roof of the laboratory, and saw...Sauron! He was winging his way toward them, with Archangel gripped tightly in his talons.

"Well, well, well," their enemy squawked as he hovered in the sky above them. "What have we here? Rebellion?"

"The flyboy doesn't look too badly hurt," Wolverine commented.

"My, what sharp eyes you have, Wolverine!" Sauron screeched. "Regrettably, your compatriot's condition is about to undergo a radical change—for the worse!" And with that, he released his prey. Archangel tumbled limply earthward...

...only to be caught by Nightcrawler, who, in a burst of smoke and flame, had teleported to catch the falling Archangel! "Sadistic swine!" he called out to Sauron. "You'll not see Archangel die this day!"

Then he teleported again to carry the both of them to safety. The strain was murderous, and it left Nightcrawler barely conscious—but he didn't mind. He had saved a friend.

"I'll deal with your elfin teammate later," Sauron announced, as he prepared to attack. "He is too weak to escape—and even if he had the strength to run, where would he go? The Savage Land is mine!"

"Not so!" Storm countered. Before Sauron could strike with his irresistible hypnotic power, Storm generated a furious blizzard! Summoning all of her strength, she dropped the temperature around Sauron to far below zero, while simultaneously striking him with winds of over two hundred knots!

Sauron instantly found himself sheathed in layers of fog, snow, and ice. He shrieked in unimaginable agony, and then dropped like a stone, stunned and stuporous.

On the floor below, Colossus was waiting. He smashed the dinosaur-man across the head with his fist of steel, sending him flying right at Wolverine, who grabbed him by the tail.

"I got him, big fella!" he called to Colossus. "The sucker's crippled. Lower the boom!"

"That, my comrade, will be a pleasure!" Colossus replied, as he began to pound the

rocks that overlooked the laboratory. The rocks cascaded down—creating a landslide that buried Sauron beneath it!

And yet, incredibly, the mutant monstrosity survived. Crawling out from underneath the towering mound of rock, he faced his foes, eyes blazing with hatred.

"It is said," he rasped, "that the greatness of a being is measured in the quality of his foes. If so, our mutual glory is assured. *Your* glory, of course, will be posthumous."

But Sauron's last threat proved an empty one. The X-Men were barely able to fight after being drained of their energy. And yet Storm was able to generate one last icy blast to topple Sauron once more into the rubble.

There was a moment of silence. Then Storm walked over to the mountain of rocks where Sauron now lay. When she looked down, however, she saw, not Sauron, but the unconscious human figure of—Karl Lykos!

"Like you, Sauron," Storm said softly, "we X-Men die somewhat harder than most. And we yield not at all. You had too little power left to fend off my attack, and therefore reverted to Karl Lykos."

CHAPTER TEN

••••••••••••••••••••••••••••••

The Cure

Later, after Tanya had been restored to normal under the anxious watch of Karl Lykos, and the evil mutants placed in Ka-zar's custody, the X-Men made their good-byes.

"This must never happen again," Storm said solemnly, staring at the accelerator. "The mutant energy accelerator is too dangerous to be entrusted to *anyone* for safekeeping."

"Agreed," said Ka-zar. "Colossus, would you do the honors?"

"The deed is done, *tovarisch*," the Russian X-Man replied. And with a mighty rush, he knocked the awful machine to smithereens.

"The mutants have been reverted to their original forms—ignorant swamp savages,"

Storm said sadly. "A cruel fate, Ka-zar."

"One richly deserved, Storm," Ka-zar countered. "And necessary. Brainchild's genius could have easily recreated the device."

"What about me?" Karl Lykos asked, Tanya's hand held firmly in his. "I'm as deadly as ever. I need to absorb life energy to survive, yet taking too much transforms me into Sauron."

"We'll find an answer," Tanya told him.

"I already have," Lykos replied grimly. "Kill me."

"The guy has a point," Wolverine said. "If you're sure, Lykos, I'll do it painlessly."

"We are not executioners, Wolverine," Storm admonished. "Even for the most noble of reasons. There may still be hope. Professor Xavier believes a cure is possible."

"Suppose he's wrong?" Ka-zar asked.

"One step at a time, my friend," Storm replied. "Farewell, Ka-zar and Zabu. It has been good to see you again. Should you ever leave your Savage Land, our home is yours."

"Who knows, Ororo?" Ka-zar said with a warm smile. "I may just take you up on that."

❖   ❖   ❖   ❖   ❖   ❖   ❖

Weeks had passed, and, far to the north, at Professor Xavier's School for Gifted Youngsters, Karl Lykos was undergoing the last in a series of arduous treatment sessions.

"He is a most fascinating subject," Xavier told Tanya as they watched the procedure along with the other X-Men.

"I'm afraid I can't be that detached and clinical, Professor," Tanya said.

"I'm sorry. I know what you must be going through." Xavier paused, then proceeded with his explanation. "Karl is not a mutant. The pteranodons that attacked you and him as children, however, *were*. He was wounded; you were not. That is why only he was affected.

"The pteranodons infected Karl with a genetic virus that mutated him, beginning the process that culminated in his transformation into Sauron. I've isolated the alien element in his DNA matrix, and these treatments are designed to burn it out of him."

"You make it sound so simple," Tanya said quietly.

"I wish it were," Xavier replied. "Too much time may have elapsed. The virus may have too strong a hold on him. Eliminating it may be impossible...or it may kill him."

Tanya and the X-Men sat by anxiously. Each one wondered which self would triumph—Karl Lykos or Sauron, good or evil.

Just then a printout came from the machine next to the table Lykos lay on. As Professor Xavier read it, a broad smile spread over his face. "The tests are negative!" he exclaimed gleefully. "Karl will live, and his genetic structure registers clean! My friend," he said, addressing Lykos, "you are cured!"

"Karl! Oh, my love!" Tanya cried, embracing him. "At last we can be together—that is, if you still want me!"

"More than ever, my darling!" he replied, kissing her passionately.

"Professor—X-Men," he said, releasing Tanya, "how can I ever repay you for this gift? This is the happiest day of my life!"

"So how come everybody's standin' around yappin'?" Wolverine asked. "If we're gonna celebrate, let's do it in style!"

And that's exactly what they did.

If you liked this book, here's a taste of...

Wolverine: Duty and Honor

"You would like to claim my daughter's hand in marriage. Your arrogance is beyond belief. Our family is as noble as it is old."

Mariko kneeled in front of him. "Father, please," she pleaded. "I beg you."

"Be silent, child," he said, without giving her a glance. His eyes were locked on Logan's. "She thinks the world of you, Wolverine. Let us see you prove your worth. Face an old man in combat!" Shingen picked up a wooden sword and tossed another to Wolverine.

"Why are we using *bokan?*" said Wolverine. "These are only practice swords. Why not the real thing?"

"To be frank," said Shingen, rising in one graceful motion, "you are not worthy of a true sword."

BOOKS IN THIS SERIES

Days of Future Past

Second Genesis

Wolverine: Top Secret

The Xavier Files

The Brood

X-Men in the Savage Land

X-Tinction Agenda

Wolverine: Duty and Honor